October 7, 1992

Happy  !

I love you!

Aunt Kathy.

Michael Hague's
ILLUSTRATED
The Teddy Bears' Picnic

by Jimmy Kennedy

Henry Holt and Company ❖ New York

To Kasha—M.H.

First edition
Published by Henry Holt and Company, Inc.,
115 West 18th Street, New York, New York 10011.
Published simultaneously in Canada by Fitzhenry & Whiteside Ltd.,
91 Granton Drive, Richmond Hill, Ontario L4B 2N5.

Library of Congress Cataloging-in-Publication Data
Kennedy, Jimmy
The teddy bears' picnic / Jimmy Kennedy, illustrated by Michael Hague
Summary: A newly illustrated version of the song about teddy bears
picnicking independently of their "owners."
ISBN 0-8050-1008-4
1. Children's songs–Texts. [1. Teddy bears–Songs and music.
2. Picnicking–Songs and music. 3. Songs.] I. Hague, Michael, ill. II. Title
[PZ8.3.K383Te 1992]
782.42164'0268–dc20   91-27709

Henry Holt books are available at special discounts
for bulk purchases for sales promotions, premiums,
fund-raising, or educational use. Special editions
or book excerpts can also be created to specification.

Printed in the United States of America
on acid-free paper.∞

1 3 5 7 9 10 8 6 4 2

The Teddy Bears' Picnic

If you go down in the woods today
You're sure of a big surprise.

If you go down in the woods today
You'd better go in disguise;

For ev'ry Bear that ever there was
Will gather there for certain, because
Today's the day the Teddy Bears
Have their picnic.

Ev'ry Teddy Bear who's been good
Is sure of a treat today.

There's lots of marvelous
Things to eat,
And wonderful games to play.

Beneath the trees where nobody sees
They'll hide and seek as long
As they please,

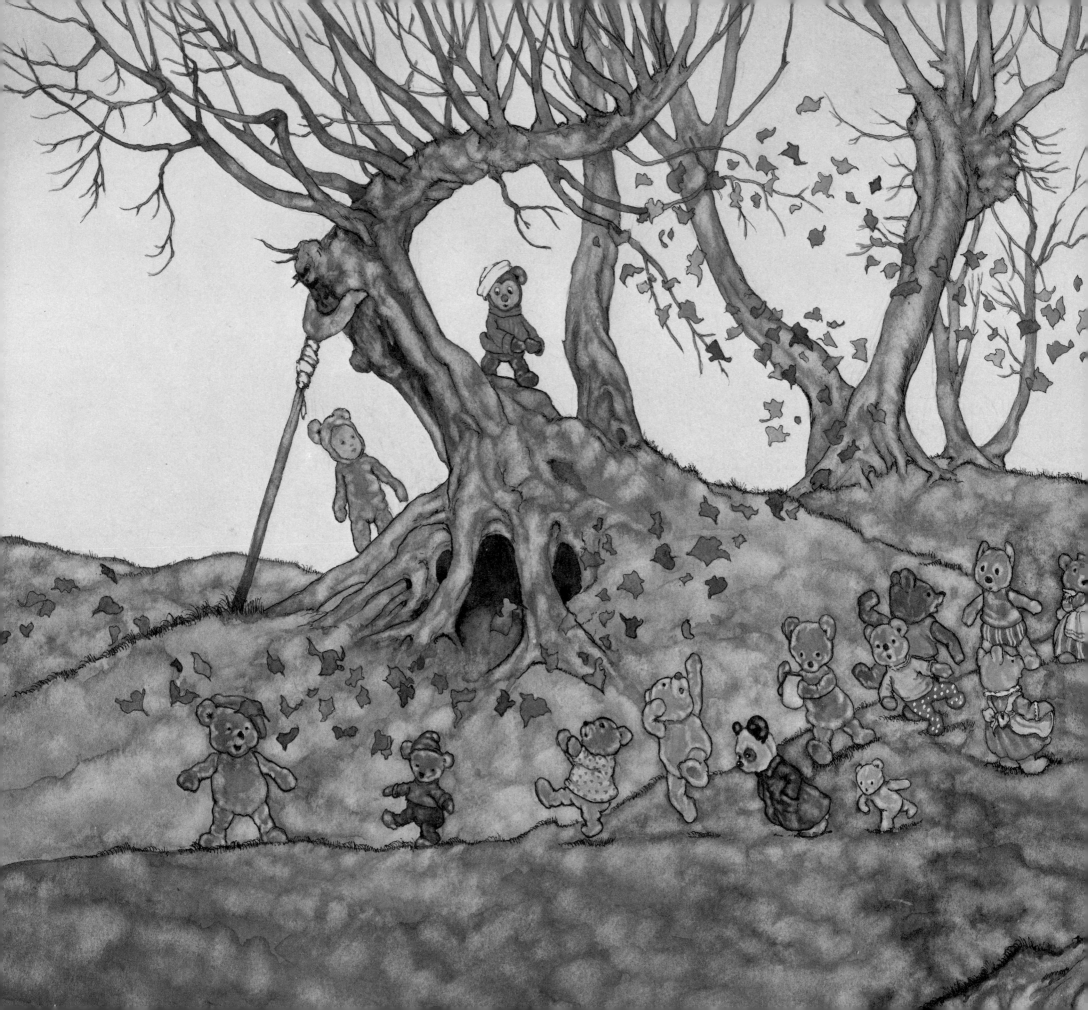

'Cause that's the way the Teddy Bears
Have their picnic.

If you go down in the woods today
You'd better not go alone.

It's lovely down in the woods today
But safer to stay at home.

For ev'ry Bear that ever there was
Will gather there for certain, because
Today's the day the Teddy Bears have
Their picnic.

Picnic time for Teddy Bears,
The little Teddy Bears are having
A lovely time today.
Watch them, catch them unawares
And see them picnic on their holiday.

See them gaily gad about,
They love to play and shout;
They never have any care;

At six o'clock their Mummies
And Daddies
Will take them home to bed,

Because they're tired little
Teddy Bears.

Books Illustrated by Michael Hague

Aesop's Fables

Alice's Adventures in Wonderland
by Lewis Carroll

Alphabears
  An ABC Book
by Kathleen Hague

Bear Hugs
by Kathleen Hague

Beauty and the Beast
Retold by Deborah Apy

A Child's Book of Prayers

Cinderella
  and Other Tales from Perrault
by Charles Perrault

Deck the Halls

The Fairies
by William Allingham

Jingle Bells

The Land of Nod
  and other Poems for Children
by Robert Louis Stevenson

Michael Hague's Favourite
  Hans Christian Andersen Fairy Tales

Michael Hague's World of Unicorns

Mother Goose
  A Collection of Classic Nursery Rhymes

The Night Before Christmas
by Clement C. Moore

Numbears
  A Counting Book
by Kathleen Hague

O Christmas Tree

Old Mother West Wind
by Thornton W. Burgess

Out of the Nursery, Into the Night
by Kathleen Hague

Peter Pan
by J. M. Barrie

The Reluctant Dragon
by Kenneth Grahame

The Secret Garden
by Frances Hodgson Burnett

The Velveteen Rabbit
  or How Toys Become Real
by Margery Williams

We Wish You a Merry Christmas

The Wind in the Willows
by Kenneth Grahame

The Wizard of Oz
by L. Frank Baum